CMP.

'Gene Kemp [is] faultless on the mysterious, transient vocabulary of the young.' *Guardian*

'Gene Kemp has addressed a wide range of readers in a variety of genres. She has proved herself to be inventive and imaginative; she is a very funny writer who writes with a passionate concern for human dignity and justice; there is a large space in her work for the underprivileged and the marginalised, and a grittiness in their representation which refuses any reader temptation to sentimentalize them.' Gillian Cross

D1147479

No Way Out

Gene Kemp grew up in Staffordshire, then studied at Exeter University. She is best known for the Cricklepit School stories, especially *The Turbulent Term of Tyke Tiler*, winner of both the Carnegie Medal and the Children's Rights Award, and which was televised and translated into many languages. Other school stories include *Gowie Corby Plays Chicken*, *Charlie Lewis Plays for Time*, runner-up for the Whitbread Award, *Juniper* and *Just Ferret*, both runners-up for the Smarties Award, *Snaggletooth's Mystery*, and *Seriously Weird*, a study of Asperger's Syndrome. Her spooky stories include *The Clocktower Ghost*, *Jason Bodger and the Priory Ghost* and *Nothing Scares Me*. *The Mink War*, a long narrative poem about mink escaping on Dartmoor, was short-listed for the Kurt Maschler Award. Gene lives in Devon and loves books and reading better than almost anything else. She also enjoys watching television, walks and talks a lot, supports Aston Villa, and really likes horrible kids.

by the same author

Bluebeard's Castle
The Turbulent Term of Tyke Tiler
Charlie Lewis Plays for Time
Gowie Corby Plays Chicken
Zowie Corby's Story
Just Ferret
Juniper
Rebel Rebel
The Clock Tower Ghost
The Tyke Tiler Joke Book
Snaggletooth's Mystery
Seriously Weird
Nothing Scares Me

NO WAY OUT

Gene Kemp

ff

faber and faber

First published in 2010
by Faber and Faber Limited
Bloomsbury House, 74–77 Great Russell Street
London, WC1B 3DA

All rights reserved
© Gene Kemp, 2010

The right of Gene Kemp to be identified as author of this
work has been asserted in accordance with Section 77 of
the Copyright, Designs and Patents Act 1988

This book is sold subject to the condition that it shall not,
by way of trade or otherwise, be lent, resold, hired out
or otherwise circulated without the publisher's prior
consent in any form of binding or cover other than that
in which it is published and without a similar condition
including this condition being imposed on the
subsequent purchaser

A CIP record for this book
is available from the British Library

ISBN 978–0–571–24455–3

2 4 6 8 10 9 7 5 3 1

No Way Out

Right from the time we set off I was scared. Scared rotten. But I didn't want to let on to Alex. He claims he's not scared of anything – anything at all. Crazy kid.

CHAPTER ONE

I wish I was back home doing stuff on the computer, my twin brother Alex's voice came into my head as we drove along in the back of Dad's car on that sunny August day.

Dad won't let us stay home by ourselves so you're stuck with it, I thought back.

Don't see why. We're twelve years old, aren't we?

We aren't identical twins – in fact Alex was born ten minutes before me and looks like Dad with fair hair and blue eyes while I'm like Mum, dark eyes, black hair. Alex is always going on about being ten minutes older and making out he's cleverer, taller, stronger, braver, better than me, more streetwise etc, etc, etc. Alex alpha, Adam beta, he chants over and over. And he calls me kid as if I was five years old and he was fifty. I yell it's more like good twin/bad twin – me good, him bad. Then we scrap and Dad goes ballistic.

But there's more than that. We've got some-thing different. Holds us together even when we argue and fight – something that we know about and no one else does, except Mum, maybe – and perhaps, though Alex won't admit it – our kid sister Emmy. 'She doesn't count, anyway,' Alex says, 'and it's our secret so don't tell – not anyone, NOT ANYONE. Or you die, kid! Promise! No tell!'

We're telepathic.

I was hearing him now.

I hate family holidays, especially at Uncle Ben's and Aunt Sadie's smelly old farmhouse with her horrible kids, Fat Bum Kelly and Spaced Out Briony and those two nerds Josh and Neville. I hate the countryside. I'm a townie, I can't be bothered with all this nature stuff. Cows, sheep, pigs, horses. Come to think of it, all that lot are just like horses!

He whinnied. Horrible.

You don't like our cousins much, do you?

How did you guess. I'm not like you. Creep.

So?

4

He's right. I like visiting them and their farm. I like the animals and the different life. We're twins, Alex and me, telepathic twins. But we're opposites, oil–water, chalk–cheese, whatever. He went on whingeing. *It's gonna drive me crazy spending two weeks out there. Why can't we go on wicked holidays if we have to go somewhere? My friends go to places like Disneyworld not some crappy old farm. I'd almost rather be in school. That's more fun.*

Just then Mum turned round in the front seat.

'You two are awfully quiet. Are you all right? Alex? Adam? You're not car sick, are you?'

'No, Mum. We're fine,' I said.

I feel sick, but not from the car, thought Alex.

'You're looking forward to seeing Uncle Ben and Aunt Sadie and your cousins again, aren't you?' asked Dad at the wheel.

'Yeah, sure,' I replied. Alex didn't bother to speak.

'Alex?'

'Yes, Dad, I'm really looking forward to seeing them all again. I've missed them so much,' he said in his most sarcastic voice. It wouldn't have done him any good complaining to Dad anyway. He'd already tried that.

'Can't I just stay at home?' he'd pleaded before.

Dad switched on the radio and his favourite music, country and western, came burbling out.

'I like this song, don't you, Liz?' he said to Mum.

Alex groaned and covered his ears.

Last time I slept in that rotten farmhouse, he thought to me, *I was nearly bitten by a rat. I woke up face to face with it. I hate that place.*

One rat going for another rat, crossed my mind, but I deleted it before Alex could read it. We only read each other's minds if we want to which is a good thing as otherwise we'd never have any privacy. If he got on my nerves too much I could block him out if I wished, as he does to me if I dare to disagree with him.

'I'm glad you don't mind going. It makes Emmy very happy. She loves it there,' said Mum.

At the mention of her name Emmy, who'd been sleeping beside us at the back stirred in her special car seat and made her happy mewing sounds. She's a very pretty girl, eight years old, with bright blue eyes and fair hair like Alex, but with a smudgy look. But she's got funny little legs and bony knees and twisty feet and can't walk properly. Something had gone wrong with her birth, Mum told us. Alex can't stand her. Mental age of about three, Alex thought to me more than once. He says she gets on his nerves, but I think he's just jealous that everyone makes a fuss of her instead of him and if anyone says she looks like him, he goes ballistic.

'You were born angry,' I said.

'That's because you were right behind me pushing me out of the way. Like always.'

'Liar,' I yelled. 'You always do what YOU want! I'm only the backup!'

So we then had a scrap. Like always.

But I was fond of Emmy, despite Alex. She's OK, actually, with her funny ways. She looked round and clapped her hands. Like always.

'You all right, Emmy?' asked Mum. 'Do you want me to sit at the back with you?'

'No, I'm OK, Mummy. With Adam.'

'So – I don't exist,' Alex muttered. 'Not that I care.'

'Where are we?' she asked in her strange little voice, like a kitten miaowing.

'We're going to see Uncle Ben and Aunt Sadie and Kelly, Briony, Josh and Neville at the farm.

You remember?'

'Oh, yes, yes. I like them. They play with me.'

'You rode on a horse last time, didn't you?'

She thought for a moment, then beamed and said, 'Yes, yes. I love horses.'

Oh, shut up, you silly little girl, thought Alex. *It's because of you I'm stuck with going to that rotten farm. You always get your own way. I wish you hadn't been born. Now just go back to sleep.*

I ignored him. I didn't like Alex when he was in one of his nasties like now.

But Emmy didn't go back to sleep. Instead she picked up a copy of *Charlotte's Web* on the seat beside her.

'Read story to me?' she asked me.

'OK.' I opened the book and started to read. Alex groaned and turned on his iPod to drown out the sound of me reading and Dad's country and western. We zoomed along with the car eating up the miles. *Soon be there* (Me). *Worse luck* (Alex).

But Alex couldn't stay quiet for long. Banging out the rhythm on his knees he started to rap loudly, drowning out *Charlotte's Web* and the sound of Kenny Rogers singing.

'Why don't you belt up?' yelled Dad, half turning in his driving seat.

'Look out!' cried Mum, and we drove into a wall of white cotton mist rising up in front of us. Dad swerved, tyres screeched and the car slid into a skid all over the road. Alex shouted and Emmy cried while Dad, like a racing driver, pulled and turned the car around, wheels spinning, tyres burning, almost out of control.

CHAPTER TWO

We ground to a halt and Dad switched on the fog lights, cutting through the murky gloom.

'Where did that come from?' he cried. 'It was fine a minute ago! Are you OK, everybody? Shut up, Alex. I know what I'm doing. I don't need you to tell me.'

'Do you know where we are, Jack?'

'I ought to. We've done this run a fair few times,' he snapped, 'but not in a fog like this.'

'Nasty white stuff. Don't like,' murmured Emmy.

'Have you got your satnav on, Dad?' asked Alex. 'That'll find the way for us.'

'Errr . . . I didn't bring it. It sent me the wrong way through a river the last time I used it.'

'Oh, great,' said Mum. 'We might end up in the middle of nowhere.'

'Well, the weather forecast never said anything about fog,' said Dad. 'And I'm pretty sure I know the way. We'll continue along this road, just go a lot slower now.'

So we crawled along through the thick enveloping fog with the car lights trying to shine a path for us. Dad peered into the gloom like a blind mouse, shoving his face right up to the windscreen and honking his horn from time to time. It was a country road and there were few other vehicles about. But it was so spooky, as if we were on an alien planet. Trees loomed up suddenly, weird, menacing shapes leaning out of the mist reaching out as if to grab us. It had been warm when we set out but now I was shivering.

'Dad – Dad – Dad,' stuttered Emmy.

'What is it, Emmy love? You OK?'

'I'm all right, thank you. I've got Adam.' She beamed at me, clutching at my arm, *Charlotte's Web* forgotten. I was wiping the windows madly trying to see where the heck we were heading for – the ditch probably.

On we slowly went, hoping the fog would ease

up soon. But it didn't. If anything, it was getting worse. Everyone was getting edgy, especially Dad.

'Who's kicking the back of my seat?' he hissed. 'If it's you, Alex, pack it in or I shall dump you on the road and leave you there stuck in the middle of nowhere.'

'It's not me. It's Adam,' he said.

'No, it isn't! You liar!'

'It's you, Adam.'

'No, it's you, Alex.'

'No – I'll tell the truth. It was Emmy.'

'With her legs, bless her? Stop it and behave yourselves,' cried Mum. 'You're not making things any better.'

We drove along in silence. I stared out at the fields shrouded in the creeping mist with the scary feeling crawling up inside me again. I didn't like this at all. Something was wrong. Yes, the fog, but something more than that, something behind the fog, threatening, menacing, evil. I wished we were back home. Instead here we were driving along in this fog nightmare, vulnerable, like lost children, defenceless as Emmy, surrounded by an alien mist.

Alex's thoughts came into my wavelength.

Adam?

Yeah.

Are you . . . scared?

Yeah, but I didn't think much ever scared you.

I know . . . but I don't like this.

'Come on, everybody,' sang Dad suddenly from the front. 'Cheer up.'

'What the heck do we have to cheer up for?' growled Alex.

'Because the fog is going away. Look.'

A wind sprang up and the mist vanished as suddenly as it had appeared, as if it had never existed. Everything was clear and green all around us. We could see where we were.

We'd arrived at the top of a hill, and in the large field beside us was a raised circle with bumps and hillocks marking the quarters. And in the middle of this circular bank stood a grey stone castle.

CHAPTER THREE

Dad pulled into a tiny parking space beside a gate and an iron fence. The sun was shining. It was warm. The fog we'd come through seemed a million miles away.

'Let's stop here for a minute. We'll get out and stretch our legs. I've never been past here before and I don't know exactly where we are. We must have gone the wrong way in that fog. I want to look at the map.'

'But it's beautiful here!' exclaimed Mum. 'I'm glad you found it.'

Emmy clapped her hands. 'Picnic. Picnic.'

It felt great to be out of the car. Alex was over the fence in a flash cos he always liked being first with me following behind. Dad lifted Emmy in her collapsible wheelchair we called the Emmy-mobile over the fence, and Mum fetched a carrier bag with food and drinks she'd brought with us for the journey.

'Come on. Race you round the bank,' Alex called to me. So we ran round the circle over the lumps and bumps, racing each other, Alex desperate to beat me cos he can't bear ever coming second. He tried to jump one of the hillocks and slipped, rolling down the bank.

'Alex. Don't roll down the banks. You'll be filthy,' said Mum.

Emmy clapped her hands and laughed.

'Dirty Alex,' she said. 'Dirty Alex.'

Glaring, he grabbed the Emmymobile and raced her round and round while she laughed and clapped her hands. He started to go faster and faster. He'd got his wicked look on . . .

'Careful,' Mum called out, but he only went faster. I jumped in front of him and held out my arms.

'Cool it, Alex!'

'Don't tell me what to do!'

He raced full speed at me to make me jump out of the way but I stayed put and at the last minute he swerved and brought the Emmy-mobile to a halt. Emmy was laughing her head off.

Dad joined us from where he had been reading the notice.

'Funny Alex tried to run me over Adam,' Emmy said, but Dad wasn't listening.

'The mounds are Neolithic,' he said. 'That means two to three thousand years old. Not the castle. That's Norman. I wonder why they built it inside these bumps.'

'To be safe, of course,' Mum said, busily doling out food, which we ate on the car blankets.

'Probably a moat round it once.' The castle had really intrigued Dad. 'Look, it's on a hill. The ground slopes away. They built it here so they could see the enemy.'

'That's Emmy. She's the enemy. Bang-bang – you're dead.'

'Stop it, Alex!'

'Funny Alex,' she said in her kitten voice.

'Who wants the last banana?' asked Mum. 'We've finished the lot then. Good . . . might be ages before we get much else to eat.'

Afterwards we explored the ruined castle; parts of the walls and battlements were still standing. As we rushed through the ruined rooms we came across an old tomb. It was covered in moss and lichen, but, picking away at it, I could see some writing.

'Wonder who it belongs to?' I said, as letters started to show up.

'Looks like L something E something Q something V something. Then N something R something. I can't make out the smaller letters.'

'Well, that tells us a lot. There's a date – August 21st. It'll be when they were born or died. They must've lived here.'

'Suppose so!' Alex shrugged.

As I picked at the moss on the old mildewed tomb I got that uneasy feeling I'd had before in the fog. Like someone or something was watching us. I looked across the field to see an old woman standing by the fence staring fixedly at us. She scared me. It felt weird. Alex had noticed, too.

'Who's that spooky-looking old bat looking at?' Alex asked. 'Mum, Dad, somebody's watching us.'

'Where, dear?' asked Mum.

'Over by the fence.'

But by the time they looked round the figure had vanished.

'Come on, time to get going,' Dad called out, 'if we want to reach the farm before midnight.'

We followed him back to the car. Alex was getting impatient as Dad consulted the map.

'I can't see this ancient monument on it,' he said at last, 'but I think if we carry on along this road we'll be going the right way.'

We all clambered in and started off again, Dad going faster than before, anxious to make up for lost time. Then we drove around a bend and there was the old woman standing in the middle of the road, staring at us with her spooky eyes. I could see her sharp, pointed, witchy face. Dad swerved, tyres screeched and the car skidded again, wheels spinning, this time really out of control, into a ditch by the side of the road.

CHAPTER FOUR

I shot out of my seat and went sprawling into Alex. The two airbags at the front opened, enveloping Mum and Dad. Emmy started screaming her head off in the back.

'Emmy. Emmy! Are you OK?' Mum shrieked.

Luckily, Emmy had been securely strapped in so she was undamaged. Wish I could say the same for my head which had banged into Alex's head. I rubbed it and could feel a lump was coming up already. The same with Alex.

Dad, you're a rotten driver, I thought, as I rubbed my head.

I dunno how he ever passed his driving test, thought Alex, rubbing his.

'Could you two help me move the car out

of the ditch?' Dad asked us.

So we all got out, leaving Emmy sitting on the back seat. The woman had vanished. She hadn't stuck around to see if we were all right, I thought. Alex's thoughts were the same, but the words in his mind were much worse than mine.

Mum stayed behind the wheel to steer while we pushed from behind. The car moved to and fro but we couldn't budge it.

'Come on, you two, put your backs into it,' demanded Dad.

I rubbed my lumpy head and then all together we produced a superhuman effort. The car shot forward suddenly. Dad and I managed to stay upright but Alex slipped and fell in the ditch. I laughed like a drain at his mad muddy face.

'Don't say anything or I'll exterminate you!' he yelled.

'It could have been worse,' I said. 'It hasn't been raining much recently.'

'Oh, great. That makes me feel so much better.'

He wiped off the mud glaring at me.

'Poor sore Alex,' murmured Emmy, and got, 'Shuddup, moron.'

Dad was back in the car now turning the ignition

key. A horrible cranking rattling sound came out. He tried again and it sounded even worse. The time after – nothing.

'I think the engine's gone. Not good. Something is seriously wrong.'

'What do you think it is?' asked Mum.

'Who knows? I'm not a mechanic. Who on earth was that woman who appeared out of nowhere?'

'We saw her back at the old castle. You should've just run her over. Then we wouldn't be in this mess,' said Alex.

'Look, if you can't say anything useful . . .' started Dad, really fed up.

Mum grabbed his arm. 'Why not phone the breakdown people?' she said. 'And Uncle Ben. Tell him we're going to be late.'

'Do you think they'll be able to find us here in the back of beyond? I don't know where we are.'

'They should be able to trace you by your mobile. Global positioning and all that,' said know-all Alex.

'OK. Let's give it a try.' He dialled the breakdown number. Nothing happened. He cursed and tried again.

'No signal. Adam, Alex, have you got your phones?'

'Yes, Dad.'

But there was no joy.

'Must be a dead zone round here or whatever,' Alex said. 'Would be, wouldn't it?'

Dad sighed deeply.

'Let's nip up the road and see if there's anything nearby – a village or town?' said Mum.

'OK.'

Race you down the lane, thought Alex.

So we raced each other down the lane, Mum and Dad following with Emmy, until we came to a junction with a sign on it, leaning on a broken stone wall. Two black and white magpies flew off as we arrived.

'What does it say?' I asked. Alex had got there first. I let him win just to get him in a good mood.

'Myton Neveridge quarter of a mile. That's not far.'

'C'mon, then.'

We rushed back to bring the good news.

'Mum, Dad. There's a village only a quarter of a mile away. We can get help there.'

Mum raised her eyes skywards. Thanks, she breathed.

So we all headed down the lane to this place called Myton Neveridge.

CHAPTER FIVE

Myton Neveridge rose out of the countryside like something out of the mists of time. Yellow-grey-brown buildings were squashed beneath roofs covered with mossy mounds and fat chimneys. The cobbled streets were rough to walk on, covered with mud and, 'Urgh – horse poo,' said Alex.

Spooky. Weird. Dontcha think, kid. Something stinks about Myton Neveridge – it's all that muck on the roads . . .

'What an amazing place. Wonderful,' gasped Mum. 'Straight out of Jane Austen.'

'It's not wonderful. It's horrible. All these awful old buildings. I like modern places, not this old dump!'

'Alex! You've no poetry in your soul!'

I kept quiet. I'd got creepy-crawlies. I didn't like Myton Neveridge. Dad walked ahead of us, trying to steer the Emmymobile over the cobbles without bumping Emmy too much. We followed.

I'd never seen anywhere so grey – no colour anywhere, only grey-yellowy brown. No one was about, no cars, no people. You couldn't see the sky as the streets were narrow and the tops of the houses and shops hung over so much it seemed as if they'd drop on us.

'Amazing,' murmured Mum.

'The name of this street is Pie Lane,' I said.

'What about this one going off it, Bladder Street. That your poetry, Mum?' Alex said.

'Must be a pedestrian area from the look of it,' Dad said.

'I wish I could have a cup of tea. I'd murder for a cup of tea.'

'You'll probably have to in this place, Mum,' answered Alex.

'Happy place.' Emmy was clapping her hands. 'Emmy Town.'

Alex: *There, Adam, I told you she was bonkers. Emmy Town! That just about fits.*

Out loud he said, 'Can't we stop? What are we looking for?'

'Somewhere or someone to tell us where we can get the car fixed. You don't suppose I want to be walking along this dreary street pushing Emmy, do you?' said Dad, getting more irritable by the minute. I hoped he and Mum weren't going to have one of their rows.

'I knew this holiday would be crap,' Alex said.

'Stop moaning. You push Emmy for a while, while I try to find somebody.'

'No way. Adam will.'

'Nice Adam. Funny Alex,' crooned Emmy, clapping her hands. 'We're in Emmy Town, y'know.'

'Oh, shut up,' Alex muttered as I took over the Emmymobile.

We walked on down the narrow winding secretive streets till we came to a crossroads in a wider space with an old grey stone cross in the middle.

Alex: *Bring on the zombies and the living dead.*

Me: *Looks that way.*

Alex: *You should like it. It's the sort of stuff you draw in your pictures at school.*

Me: *Doesn't mean I like it. Scares me rotten.*

Alex: *You're always scared. Wimp.*

Dad stood still, sighing, 'Now which way?'

'You've got a choice. Scissors Street, Cheeke Street, Old Way . . .' Mum read out.

'Old Way!' echoed Emmy. 'Go Old Way, Dad-Dad.'

That was her baby name for him.

Alex rolled his eyes and groaned.

'We might as well go that way as any . . .' Mum put in, so on we trundled, Alex muttering, Dad striding on ahead. We went down one street, then another. No one was about. No traffic. No animals. A dead town. A ghost town. I knew Dad was getting angry and guessed he'd explode any minute, then suddenly he turned round and called, 'Look. There's a pub. The Hanley Arms. I thought there'd be one somewhere. Everywhere has one . . .'

' . . . even Myton Neveridge . . .' said Alex.

Sounds of life came from inside. Oh, good, Myton Neveridge isn't completely dead, I thought as we went through a narrow hall into a dark room. An enormous stag with glassy eyes and swooping antlers hung above the biggest fireplace you ever saw.

Me: *They're big into hunting here.*

Alex: *Hope they don't want to kill us.*

The room was full of gloomy corners, blurry pictures and old furniture. The noise and chatter stopped as we shuffled over the reeds and grass on the floor.

'Can't even afford carpets,' muttered Alex.

Everyone turned round and stared at us, thin faces, no smiles, just wooden, stony cold expressions.

I wanted to disappear, become invisible, anything.

I reached out for Alex in my head.

Where are we?

In the film Shaun of the Dead *only it's Us and the Dead. Hope they eat Emmy first and keep us for afters. That'll give time for someone to rescue us.*

In complete silence Dad headed for the bar. It had two small barrels on it, loads of bottles and jugs and dull metal mugs and glasses. A bald-headed man stood there beside a young thin dark-haired woman in a long dress.

'Can I have a pint of your best, please?' Dad asked the barman, who was eyeing us like we were Martians. Dad's got guts. I just wanted to run. So did Alex.

Mum pushed Emmy forward.

'Are children allowed in here?' she asked nervously and Emmy whispered in her funny miaow voice, 'Please, Emmy wants a drink.'

It was like the sun breaking through. Suddenly all the people were smiling, talking and all looking at Emmy as if she was . . .

Best thing since sliced bread, thought Alex.

From the shadows spoke a big booming voice and out stepped a tall thin man. He had a ginger beard and was dressed like Robin Hood in a leather jerkin and cords.

'Alfred. Tess, come on, serve these good people. Where's your hospitality?'

'Yes, sir,' said Alfred the barman and began to pour Dad's pint into a metal mug.

'What would 'ee like?' asked Tess, the dark-haired girl, winking and smiling at Emmy.

The mug she gave her was special. Silver, I guessed. Not like ours.

The man dressed like Robin Hood came over and joined us.

'Forgive our bad manners,' he said. 'It's just that

we're not accustomed to strangers visiting in these parts.'

'I'm not surprised,' muttered Alex, under his breath.

'Let me introduce myself. I'm Robert Hanley ... and you are?'

Dad gave our names.

'Where have you come from?' asked Mr Hanley.

'Well, we were driving through the country-side on our way to visit our relatives when we got lost in the fog and our car broke down.'

I suddenly remembered the cause of our accident, the old witchy woman, and I looked round the pub to see if she was there. But there was no sign of her.

'We tried to ring the breakdown service, but our mobiles wouldn't work. Do you have a telephone we could use?'

Mr Hanley looked sadly at us and shook his head.

I looked out of the pub window to see if there were any telephone lines but there weren't any. He was right.

Alex's thoughts suddenly went into overdrive.

No telephones!! What's the matter with this place? Everybody's got telephones! Are these people living in a time warp?

I tried to block out his thoughts cos I was interested in what people were doing and saying. I could listen to Alex any time. Robert Hanley was still speaking, 'I'm sure our village handyman John will be able to mend your cart if you tell him where it is. He's a very capable man, though making cartwheels is more his forte. I'm sure he can fix it for you.'

I don't believe it. No cars! came Alex again, sounding like someone off the telly whose name I can't remember. That was something else missing when we walked up the street. No cars.

You can carry being green too far, Alex thought at me.

'John,' Mr Hanley called to a stocky man who was sitting by the bar drinking, 'these good people have a vehicle broken down just outside the village. Can you go and deal with it?'

'Yes, sir,' he replied, and he left the pub without finishing his drink. Robert Hanley was certainly the boss in these parts, I thought. He probably owns the pub as well, surprise, surprise, since it

34

was called The Hanley Arms, and everything else in the village.

'You must be famished,' he said. 'I'll find you a table and we'll bring you some food.'

'Thank you,' said Dad.

'You're very kind,' said Mum.

He ushered us over to a table hidden away in the dark corner.

Alex: *Bet the grub's gross. Don't fancy it.*

We were served by a big gangly youth, all limbs, who accidentally banged into Alex's chair as he waited on us. 'Retard,' Alex muttered under his breath, 'he should be called Lurch.' He was doing his best as usual to get on with everyone. I think the boy heard him because he didn't look too pleased.

Alex was right about the food. One piece of meat and bits of old veg and weeds floated in a pool of grey sludge. A blackish lump of bread hung over the side of the plate.

'What is it?' asked Alex.

'Rabbit,' the boy Lurch answered, smiling evilly. Alex turned green.

We'd eaten the picnic grub so we weren't starving which was just as well as we couldn't finish this awful meal. The boy cleared the table away, still smiling.

I noticed that other people had gathered round and were watching us.

'Prize exhibits,' muttered Alex.

They seemed to take a particular interest in Emmy. Tess couldn't keep her eyes off her.

'What a pretty little girl,' they said.

'Lovely little girl.'

'Lovely, lovely little girl.'

'Lovely, lovely, lovely little girl.'

Emmy was lapping it all up and beaming and clapping happily. 'Nice people,' she smiled. She looked very little and pretty with all the old, thin, bony, wrinkled faces around her. Their voices were strange, soft, slow.

What odd voices, Alex's thoughts came over. *Thickies.*

'Pity about 'er legs, but 'er's still beautiful,' one murmured, putting out a hand to pat her hair.

Alex made the occasional sick noise under his breath. I was just glad nobody wanted to pat our hair, especially as Alex was scowling at everything.

CHAPTER SIX

'Time to be going, I think,' said Dad. 'Can you give me the bill, please?'

'A guinea, sir,' said Alfred the barman.

'You're joking.'

'No. It's not too much, is it, sir?'

'N-n-no.'

Dad fished around, looking rather bewildered, then triumphantly came up with a pound coin and some ten pences. Alfred put them all in a wooden box on the table.

Mr Hanley's voice rang out again as we headed for the door.

'You're not leaving us, are you? It's getting late and you've broken down. You must stay here tonight. I think they have a spare room.'

'No . . . really . . .'

'No buts . . . I insist. A good night's sleep and you can be on your way in the morning. John will have fixed your carriage by then.'

'Well . . . thank you,' said Mum. 'You're very good, very kind.'

We followed Alfred up the narrow twisting wooden stairs to a large panelled room, with heavy beams on the ceiling. There was a large bed with curtains round it hung on four posts and a little bed at the foot. A basin and jug stood on a kind of chest with a scrawny-looking piece of cloth on it. In a connecting room just off, I could see two beds also with curtains round them side by side, for me and Alex probably. Strange – it was as if they knew we were coming. I bounced on one of them. It was hard and felt as if it had been stuffed with straw. *I bet it has fleas. Yuck,* I thought. I pushed that idea to the back of my mind for I didn't like it much. Alex appeared, groaning . . .

'Where did you go, Alex?'

'I now know where the word bog comes from. That's what they use for a toilet. A bog or swamp. Makes our school bogs look like the latest in technology. It's certainly medieval.'

I went to find out if he was right. It was down the end of the corridor. He was right. I'd never seen anything like it.

We looked round our rooms. There were no modern appliances of any kind, only oil lamps. I guessed there was no electricity.

'I see they've got no television,' Alex said. 'I don't believe these people! How can they live like this? It's unreal. No cars, telephones, computers, proper toilets. What an awful place! Even Uncle Ben's rotten farm has a telly. What do they do for entertainment round here?

Talk about grumpy old men on the telly, Alex is a grumpy young one, I thought.

'Oh, do be quiet, Alex,' snapped Mum. 'Not everybody in the world wants the same lifestyle as you, thank heavens.'

'But there's nothing to DO! I can't just sit here doing NOTHING!'

'You could try going to sleep. It's been a long day,' said Dad wearily.

'But it's still light! I can't go to sleep yet!'

'What's the time, then?' I asked.

'Dunno. My watch has stopped,' said Alex.

'So's mine,' said Mum.

'I knew it. They've all stopped. This place is haunted!'

'Don't talk rubbish! I don't want Emmy frightened.'

Emmy didn't look frightened. She'd pulled herself on to her bed and was humming a little song:

'Rock a bye Emmy
on the soft bed
Don't let her tumble or
we'll all be dead!'

'Her bed's all silk,' exclaimed Mum, patting it.

'Oh, for Pete's sake,' yelled Alex. 'Let's get out of here!'

'We'll be out of here tomorrow. You can put up with this for one night!'

'No, I can't. Dad, let's go for a walk. Take a look round. See if we can contact anybody, Uncle Ben or Missing Persons!'

'OK,' he said, after a minute.

And so there we were walking through Myton Neveridge with the Emmymobile rattling on the cobbles. We'd managed to slip out without being noticed, good. We didn't need another conversation with Robert Hanley, Sir, or Alfred the barman.

Alex: *I wonder if there's a Tesco here.*

Me: *Doesn't seem likely.*

Alex: *Nor a Pound Stretcher.*

Me: *Maybe they don't need one.*

Alex: *What d'you mean?*

Me: *I dunno.*

Alex: *You mean it's weird here.*

Me: *Yeah. You could say that. There's something strange happening here – and we're stuck in the middle of it.*

Alex: *You think something will happen, don't you?*

Me: *Yes, I do.*

Alex: *Are we in danger, here?*

Me: *Shuddup. Look, people are coming out . . .*

Alex: *And they're all looking at us!*

It was true. The streets of Myton Neveridge were filling up with people, old people, young people, children, walking along, thin, lined hungry-looking people in raggedy grey garments. No animals. Where were the animals?

Eaten, thought-waved Alex. *I'm just scared they'll eat us next.*

'I don't think I like this much,' Mum said. 'It's like a sort of wasteland. Can't we go back in?'

But Emmy was smiling and clapping her hands. A little singing sound came from her chair. 'Emmy happy,' she crooned.

The people all looked at her, smiling and laughing with her. They formed a procession round us and behind us. Tess from the Hanley Arms was suddenly there, walking beside Emmy, smiling down at her and at us. Emmy waved her hands at them like royalty.

'Oh, for heaven's sake, let's get back to the Hanley Arms,' snapped Dad, seizing Emmy and her chair off Mum and turning round. It wasn't easy since three people and Tess were holding bits of it and trying to touch Emmy's hair.

Alex: *If this is what being a pop star's like, I won't bother. I don't want to be a celebrity, thank you, I'll tell my fan club.*

He grinned fiercely at everyone but no one took any notice of him. They were completely focused on Emmy. Only Tess looked at us at all. On we went . . .

Me: *Dad must have taken the wrong turn . . .*

Alex: *He always takes the wrong turn . . .*

For we came down a street that ended − oh, no, no, no, no − in a wall of fog, thick as a white blanket.

'Not that way,' smiled Tess who might have been very pretty except for a black tooth at the front. 'There's no way that way.'

Somehow we turned the Emmymobile, then with what looked like the entire population of Myton Neveridge, headed in another direction, Emmy singing and clapping in her chair.

'She's so pretty,' someone was saying. 'You must love her so much.'

'Yes,' said Mum feebly above the singing.

'We shall love her so much,' went on the speaker.

'We all love her so much,' the crowd murmured.

On we walked, not getting any nearer to the Hanley Arms. We passed another church. There were a lot of churches, it seemed. Grey, grim churches. With gargoyles. I didn't want to look at them.

'I can bear this as long as I don't look at their

awful faces,' Alex's voice sounded desperate.

'I'd like to walk right out of here,' Dad muttered, but no way. This time a pair of huge wooden doors that looked as if they wouldn't open in a million years loomed before us. They were stuck into high grey town walls. No go, this way.

We were turned round by the crowd. We couldn't stop them. We now knew we had no say in where we were going. We were in their hands. The hands of Myton Neveridge.

'Please take us back to the Hanley Arms,' Mum's voice wobbled a bit.

'The mist is bad tonight,' said Tess. 'There's just one more way to try.'

This time we were taken as far as the edge of Myton Neveridge where there were no more houses and shops, and fields lay in front of us.

And a river. A wide, fast-flowing river lay between us and the outside world. Fat, white, cotton-wool mist hung over it. A ring of bells sounded from the church looming above us.

Alex: *Another fog! Another church!*

As if in answer all the other churches rang their bells. The air was filled with sound all around us.

Emmy's face was radiant, beaming as we all stood still. They wouldn't let us move.

Alex: *We're prisoners, Adam. I shall go mad.*

Me: *Me, too. Won't they ever stop?*

At that moment the bells stopped. The silence was like velvet.

'Emmy happy. Pretty Emmy,' she sang, clapping her hands.

'Pretty Emmy. Happy Emmy,' the people sang in chorus.

'We'll take you back now,' said Robert Hanley, appearing out of nowhere, 'and you can get some sleep. I think you need it.'

In minutes we were back at the Hanley Arms. Alfred the barman had a warm drink ready for us, a whitish liquid. I hoped it was milk, but I was so thirsty I didn't really care. I was exhausted and could hardly even think.

It seemed in no time we were in bed and as I drifted off to sleep, I heard Alex say,

'I don't think Myton Neveridge is real, kid, but right now I can't . . .'

CHAPTER SEVEN

I was the first to wake up, wondering where on earth I was. I looked round and the dream/nightmare was still here. I gazed up at the wall behind my bed and a picture caught my eye. It was a portrait of a very pretty woman with a caption underneath – Lady Eleanor, Queen of the Village. She wore a scarlet dress and a cloak of shining grey velvet, and her hair was golden. Looking closely at it, I was reminded of someone. Yes, Emmy. Lady Eleanor looked like a grown-up version of Emmy. They had the same hair, eyes, everything. Maybe that was why those people were making such a fuss of her last night, calling her lovely and all that.

Dad awoke next and clapped his hands together.

'Come on, everybody. Get up. Let's get cracking. I don't know the time and I don't want to be here any longer than I have to.'

'Nor me,' groaned Alex, sleepily. 'I'd hoped that yesterday had been just a nightmare, but I'm really here.'

Everyone was soon rushing about getting dressed and gathering things together, Mum helping Emmy. I tried to point out the picture, but nobody was interested.

We all headed downstairs. Alfred was behind the bar cleaning some metal mugs. Dad went up to him.

'Can I have the bill, please?'

'Why. You're not leaving, are you?'

'Yes, thank you.'

'All right then. If you're sure you're not staying another night?'

'No, we're not.'

'What about some breakfast?' asked Alex.

'We'll get some food later,' Dad said irritably. 'I want to be on our way. Let's find that garage and see if the car's ready.'

We left the pub and headed up the street. Luckily none of those people were around. We walked around till we came across a yard with a sign saying 'John's Wheelmakers'.

'This must be the place of that bloke who's doing our car,' said Dad.

'Yes, but he doesn't seem to be here,' said Mum.

We looked round but there was no sign of either John or the car, just a load of cartwheels and some other machinery and bits and pieces.

Dad paced up and down outside chewing his lip.

'I don't like this. I'm not sure if he's collected the car or if he even knows how to fix it.'

'What do you want to do, Jack?' asked Mum.

'Leave this place for a start. The road out of here must lead somewhere. There must be other villages and places not far away.'

'Good. Glad someone agrees with me,' said Alex.

'And me,' I said.

'I like it here,' piped up Emmy. 'Nice people. They love Emmy.'

'I know what's wrong with this place,' said Mum.

'Yeah. Like it's back in the Middle Ages,' said

Alex. 'A time warp. Full of mad people.'

'No, it's not that. I like the buildings. No, it's the silence. There's no sound of birds or animals or anything like that, which is strange in the countryside.'

We all stopped to listen. She was right. It was as quiet as a graveyard.

'That does it,' said Dad. 'Let's get out of here.'

We walked rapidly up the long main street, ignoring any of the side streets. A few people stopped and said 'lovely' to Emmy in the Emmy-mobile again, but we didn't hang around. Soon we found ourselves at the end of the village and in front of a signpost. Two magpies perched on it flew away as we approached. To the left it said PUMPHREY COLLETT 1½ MILES, to the right it said RAVENSCROFT 3 MILES.

'We didn't see that last night,' I said. 'I wonder why?'

'Who cares as long as we're outta here,' said Alex.

'There. That's not too far. We'll try Pumphrey Collett since it's nearer,' said Dad.

'I hope it's not like this place,' said Alex, helpful as usual.

'Surely not. It can't be this backward. Look, even if it's only got a phone box that'll be an improvement. We can contact the breakdown people and Uncle Ben.'

We left Myton Neveridge and walked along a winding country lane. After a while the sun came out and the sounds of the countryside reached our ears.

'Listen. I can hear the birds again now,' Mum sang out.

This cheered us up for a short while, but that didn't last very long. On and on the road went alongside the grey stone village wall and we didn't seem to be getting anywhere.

'It's a very long one and a half miles,' said Dad.

It was a bumpy road too and Emmy wasn't happy in the Emmymobile.

'Bumps. Emmy's bottom,' she mewed and that kick-started Alex.

'I hate the countryside. Right now, I don't think I ever want to leave our house again. Or go on holiday. Everything I need is at home. What I don't want is Myton Neveridge and all that goes with it . . .'

'Stop whingeing,' said Dad. 'We've got to get to

this other village sometime.'

On and on we went until at last we saw a sign in the distance.

'That must be it,' we called out, and got moving, this was better, this felt more like it. Hope, hope. Then we got to the sign that leaned on a broken stone wall and read the name on it. Two black and white birds flew away. I didn't like them.

Myton Neveridge.

'Oh, no!' bellowed Alex. That's exactly what I thought.

Mum groaned.

Dad put his head in his hands, then punched the air with his fist.

'I don't get it. How can we be back here?'

'Goody.' Emmy smiled. 'Back home.'

'What the heck makes you think it's home, you nutter!' yelled Alex.

'We must have gone round in a complete circle,' said Mum.

The yellow-grey village lay before us. Nearby was a large wooden seat. We headed over and sat down to rest our aching limbs except for Emmy in her Emmymobile, who was clapping her hands.

I hate her, Alex's thoughts were red, banging . . .
She's not causing this . . .
Yes, she is. It's her fault.

'Now what? Shall we try Ravenscroft?'

'Dad, it's three miles. The other one was bad enough,' said Alex. 'I'm tired.'

'Nonsense. You're young and fit. Do you the world of good.'

'No, I'm not. And I'm hungry. We didn't have any breakfast. Even if the grub's horrible here, it's better than nothing.'

'Let's get to Ravenscroft first. We can find something to eat there.'

As we started to move Emmy started struggling and crying in her seat.

'No want more ride. Want to stay here.'

'C'mon, Emmy. You'll be OK,' I said.

'Nasty bumpy road. Like it here.'

I always thought you were stupid, but I didn't know how much, Alex came through. *How can you like this place?*

We tried to push her, but she started shrieking.

'Want to go back to pub. Our place.'

Mum and Dad stopped and looked at each other.

53

'I can't take her like this, Jack. I'd better take her back to the Hanley Arms.'

'I don't want to leave you here on your own, Liz.'

'We'll be all right. The people are quite friendly and they seem to really like Emmy. They won't do anything to hurt us, I'm sure. Anyway, I don't think I'm up to walking all that distance with her.'

We watched her walking back through the village with Emmy, Dad looking worried. But what else could we do?

'Come on then, you two. Let's hit the road again. Ravenscroft, here we come.'

'Well, I hope that place is really here,' said Alex. 'Not out in some time warp.'

'Don't even think that.'

A long time later we arrived back at the signpost with aching feet. There had been no sign of Ravenscroft either. Myton Neveridge, said the signpost leaning on the broken wall. Two magpies flew away, making jeering noises.

'It just doesn't make sense,' said Dad.

'What about that road we came in on? With the castle? Where's that?' I said.

'Who knows? I can't see it. Or the castle,' said Alex, too tired to make any clever comments.

'What's happening to us, Dad?' I asked.

'I don't know.' His voice was tired. 'I don't understand it at all ...'

'We're either caught in some mad time warp or we're imagining it all,' said Alex.

'Maybe we've landed on another planet. All that mist was the gateway or something,' I said. 'Maybe a parallel universe?'

'I wish we were on a planet with better grub. I'm starving.'

'Well, let's go back to the pub and see Mum,' said Dad. 'Then we'll work out what to do next. But whatever we do, we mustn't frighten Emmy.'

Alex groaned, 'The story of my life: Don't Frighten Emmy! Here we are zipping in and out of time, into alternative parallel universes and back again, but that's OK as long as we don't frighten Emmy!'

Three weary hungry figures tottered back up the village to the Hanley Arms. Alfred was serving behind the bar.

'Hello. You've decided to come back, then.' He smiled.

'Yes, for the moment,' said Dad curtly.

'So pleased.'

'Is my wife in?'

'Yes. She's upstairs.'

We staggered up the stairs, dying for a rest, to find Mum asleep on the double bed. But Emmy was nowhere to be seen. Her bed was empty. She'd disappeared.

CHAPTER EIGHT

Dad shook Mum roughly.

'Lizzy. Wake up. Where's Emmy?'

Mum came to, slowly.

'What did you say?'

'Where's Emmy?'

Mum was suddenly wide awake.

'What? She's in her bed, isn't she?'

'No, she isn't.' We searched the room, all thoughts of tiredness gone now. But she wasn't there. Neither was the Emmymobile.

'Someone's taken her. Come on, you lot. We've got to go and find her.'

I followed Mum and Dad to the door, but Alex lay on his bed, groaning.

'You lot go and look for her. I'm too knackered.'

'ALEX! She's your sister! Don't you care about her?' shrieked Mum.

'Well, I suppose so,' he shrugged.

'Alex, if you want to stay alive for another minute . . .' said Dad threateningly.

'All right, all right, keep cool,' he muttered under his breath as he got up and joined us.

We rushed back downstairs into the pub lounge.

'Everything all right, folks?' drawled Alfred.

'No, everything is NOT all right! My daughter's missing. Where is she?'

Alfred shrugged his shoulders.

'Ain't seen 'er.'

'You must've done if you were here all the time. How could anyone come from our room without you seeing them?'

'Us weren't 'ere earlier . . . Perhaps 'er went missing then. 'Ave 'ee seen 'er, Tess?'

Tess shook her head.

'No, Alfred. I ain't seen her.'

Mum pulled Dad away as he went to take a swing at Alfred and shoved him into the street. He pushed her away.

'Get off. Why didn't you stay awake? You know

I wasn't happy about you coming back with her on your own. How could you be so careless?'

Mum's eyes filled with tears.

'I don't know. Before I went upstairs with Emmy I had a drink and then I felt really tired afterwards.'

'Someone drugged your drink, I bet,' said Alex. 'Anything's possible here.'

Dad raised his eyes to Heaven. 'I don't believe it! I just don't . . .' he spluttered with fury.

'I'm not sure,' said Mum. 'If I was drugged there were plenty of people in the pub. It could've been anyone . . .'

'What shall we do next?' I asked.

'Go and ring on every door in the village if we have to, ask if anybody's seen her.'

Dad rang on the nearest doorbell and Mum the next one and we went around in a group, asking everybody we saw. We all got the same reply. Nobody had seen her.

This is a waste of time, thought Alex to me. *Even if they've taken her, she's probably hidden down an old cellar by now. We'll never find her cos we can't search the houses. There's no police around to help either.*

We have to try, though. You don't care if she has been taken, do you?

Why? They're welcome to her. All that 'lovely little girl' stuff. They're crazy about her, anyway.

There were times – like now – when I realised what a complete rat my twin brother was. I tried to switch off from him.

Don't speak or think to me right now.

Why not? What's wrong with you? Anyway, you wouldn't have to read her any more silly stories.

I don't mind reading her stories. Now just shut up and leave me alone.

We tried house after house, the shopkeeper, butcher, baker – we'd have tried the candlestick maker if the village had one. We went down Pie Lane, Scissors Street, Cheeke Street, even Bladder Street. Dusk was falling as our search began to narrow down. Everywhere wc went – same answer. Nobody had seen her. It went on and on. Was this long awful day never going to end? Mum was white and distant, Dad red and shouty.

'What shall we do?' asked Mum wearily. 'We've tried all the houses now, I think.'

'Not quite,' said Dad. We'd reached the end of Old Way, a grander street than the others with more important-looking buildings. 'Look where we are.'

We were outside the grandest house in the village – Hanley House.

'If anyone knows what's going on it'll be him. He's the boss.'

We walked up a gravel drive and rapped on an old antique doorknob. After a moment a girl came to the door, small and tired, long skirts dragging on the stone floor.

'Is Mr Hanley in?' asked Dad.

'Eem out I'se afraid. An' tes Lord 'Anley, not Mr.'

'I might have guessed,' muttered Alex. 'But I'm not calling him Lord.'

Dad leaned against the door and groaned. This couldn't be happening. It just couldn't. Dad's tough but you could see it was all getting to him.

Then came the sound of horse's hooves and a tall imposing figure appeared on a white horse. Robert or Lord or Mr Hanley had arrived. He got down and came towards us.

'What can I do for you?' he asked in his pleasant, polite way. *Lord* Hanley was definitely posh. 'Annie, go and stable my horse, will you. You all look very tired. Would you like to come in and have some refreshment?'

We followed him inside into a huge, wonderful room full of tapestries, paintings, furniture, like an antique warehouse. I couldn't take my eyes off a full suit of armour standing in an alcove.

Alex: *This lot must be worth a fortune*

Me: *Shuddup. I don't want to talk to you.*

We sat down on a carved wooden bench. Another servant appeared.

'Go and get some tea and refreshments for my guests.'

I took a sip from a metal mug and it made me feel dizzy. Was this the drink that had sent Mum to sleep? I decided not to finish it. Dad was shifting about restlessly but you couldn't rush Mr Hanley. There was something about him, he was so in control all of the time.

Finally he turned to us sitting there with his fingers clasped together.

'Now, how can I help you then?'

'Our little girl's missing,' Mum pleaded. 'We've looked everywhere in the village, but we can't find her.'

Mr Hanley sat there with a concerned expression on his face.

'Do you know anything, sir?' Dad asked bluntly.

'No, I'm afraid I've been away from the village today. It certainly is shocking news that your daughter has gone missing. I too have had the misfortune of losing someone I cared deeply about – my dear wife Lady Eleanor in a tragic accident. I feel for you entirely.' His voice sounded like honey mixed with syrup, soothing, calming.

Lady Eleanor? That rang a bell. Of course, the picture in my bedroom in the pub! I looked round the room but couldn't see a portrait – perhaps he had one upstairs or perhaps it was too painful for him to keep one at home. I wondered what had happened to her, but didn't dare ask. Alex did, of course.

'What happened to her?'

Lord Hanley didn't reply, only sat silent and sad.

And suddenly Mum cracked,

'I think someone in the village has taken her. You've got to help us! You've got to. What are we doing here? We didn't want to come here. And we can't seem to leave. Everything's wrong. And now someone's stolen Emmy!'

'Please be calm,' said Lord Hanley.

'Can you help us find her, then?' Dad asked.

'I'm sure I can help, but it's getting very late now. I know everything that goes on in the village and I promise – no, I guarantee – that I will return your daughter to you tomorrow. Have no fears on that score.' He sounded very genuine.

Alex: *Don't believe a word. He's conning us. He knows something. He did his wife in and now he's abducted Emmy.*

Me: *I don't know what to think.*

We followed him to the front door which he opened for us. Just before we left Dad asked, 'By the way, do you know how our car's coming along? I didn't see it at John's place.'

'John has been working on it today outside the village where it crashed and he assures me that it will be ready by tomorrow. When you find your daughter you can be on your way then.'

Back at the pub we collapsed in our room. We were shattered. Everything was so horrible I didn't want to talk. I just wanted to sleep so I didn't have to think of Emmy lost and afraid without us.

'I shan't sleep a wink tonight. I'm so worried about Emmy,' said Mum.

'Try to if you can, Liz,' urged Dad. 'We need you to be alert tomorrow.'

'They've taken her. It's obvious. They were all crazy about her.'

'We need to get away from here. We've got to escape!' said Alex.

'But it's like a prison. We can't get away,' I said.

'It seems like that,' said Dad.

'We were led here so they could take Emmy ... my lovely Emmy ...'

'I reckon that old witch has something to do with this,' said Alex.

'I dunno,' I replied. 'I haven't seen her since we got here.'

'Yeah, but I bet she's around somewhere,' said Alex. 'Perhaps she's got Emmy.'

'Shut up,' I hissed, as Mum howled. 'We'll get her back, Mum ...'

'Dear Adam. You think she's all right, don't you?'

'Of course she is,' snapped Alex. 'Everyone always looks after her. She's probably gobbling tea and cakes now with everyone telling her how lovely she is.'

'Oh, I hope so, oh, I do! You'll help us find her,

won't you, Alex, you're so clever and Adam's so kind . . .'

'We'll have another go when it's light – to get out of this place, find the police, phone Uncle Ben,' said Dad. 'Now, everyone, try and get some sleep.'

CHAPTER NINE

Dad woke up first next morning and dragged me and Alex out of bed. Mum came to rather more slowly.

'I'd only just dropped off. I couldn't sleep,' she confessed.

'Right, let's find Emmy, collect the car and leave this godforsaken place once and for all,' said Dad, heading straight for the door. He turned the handle to find that it was . . . locked. He frowned and tried again. And again. It wouldn't budge. He stood there irritably for a moment, then started banging the old heavy oak door with his fists.

'What the hell's going on here? Somebody unlock this door right now! What is the meaning of this?'

We all sat there nervously as he kept on kicking and banging the thick solid door. I'd never seen him in a worse temper than he was in right now. Finally footsteps approached and a voice, Alfred the barman's, said,

'What do 'ee want?'

'What do you mean, what do I want? Why have you locked us in this room?'

'Because today's ourn Special Village Day and youm not invited. You'll just get in the way of our celebrations. I'll let you out tomorrow when 'tis all over.'

'When what's all over?'

There was no reply. We could hear footsteps walking away now.

'Come back and let us out!' Dad yelled and began banging on the door. Nothing happened. Except Dad doing more banging on the door.

Mum slumped back on to the bed.

'Will this horrible nightmare never end? Do you think this has anything to do with Emmy's disappearance?'

'Could be. Just let's get out of here.' Dad shoulder-charged the door with all his strength, but it was no use.

'I thought that would open it,' Dad groaned. 'It's solid. I think they've wedged something on the other side.'

'It wouldn't surprise me. Nothing would any more,' Mum said sadly.

'Let me have a go,' said Alex.

'Don't waste your time,' said Dad wearily.

Alex took no notice, did a short run up, leapt high in the air and attempted to kung-fu kick the door open, but just ended up rebounding back into the room.

'We need one of those enforcers like the police use to open doors,' he growled.

'Well, there doesn't seem to be one in here, does there?' Dad remarked sarcastically. 'Got any more bright ideas?'

Alex pointed out the candles and the oil lanterns.

'Set light to one of those and burn the pub down. We can escape then.'

'And burn us with it, you fool. I don't want to die.'

I noticed the portrait of Lady Eleanor again.

'It's something to do with her, I think. You look at her. She's got Emmy's face.'

Mum and Dad looked closely at the picture for the first time.

'You're right, Adam. Is that why they want Emmy?' Mum said.

'Why would they want her just cos she looks like some grotty Lady or other?' Alex put in. 'Doesn't make sense.'

'Nothing makes sense in this place,' cried Mum. 'Oh, Emmy. Where are you?'

Alex's eyes were swivelling round the room again and he pointed to the high-up window.

'That's no good,' said Dad. 'I noticed it before. I can't get through that. It's too small.'

'Neither can I,' sighed Mum.

'I think we can. Me and Adam.'

'It's too dangerous. We're too high up here,' said Mum. 'We're not on the ground floor, you know.'

'It's all right. I'm good with heights.'

Yeah, he is. Last term he climbed up on the school roof to fetch a football we'd been playing with. He was spotted and got a detention. Didn't bother Alex, though. He boasted about it for ages.

He climbed up on a chair and pushed open the window.

'It's not too high up. I can get out of there. I'll

try to find the key and let you out.

'But if I can't then you've got to try and escape. There's some fields behind the pub. With any luck nobody'll see you. Just go that way. Don't go into the village or take the road – it didn't work last time.'

'Are you sure, Alex?' said Mum. 'I don't want you getting hurt.'

'It's OK, Mum. I'm cool about it. I told you – heights don't bother me.' He wriggled through the open window and crouched on the sill. 'It's OK, look, it's not too far, cos there's a bit of roof sticking out. I can land on that and then get to the ground.'

Dad came and peered out as best he could.

'Yes, there's an extension so it's not too far down. You go with him, Adam,' urged Dad. 'He'll need you.'

I peered out through the window as Alex slith-ered down on to the flat roof. It seemed far enough to me. I wasn't as keen on heights as Alex. He'd reached the ground now and was watching from below.

Come on, you wimp, he thought at me.

So I took a deep breath, followed him out of

the window and was on the ground in a few minutes.

That was good fun. He beamed.

Yeah, if you say so.

We were right behind the pub so I looked through one of the back windows. It looked completely deserted.

'Alex?' I said, talking normally now.

'Yeah?'

'Dad told us to escape across the fields, but look, there's nobody in the pub, I think, and the key to that room might be there. We could let Dad and Mum out.'

'OK. Let's give it a go.'

So we slipped into the pub through the back door, ready to run if we saw anybody. But it was OK. Nobody was there.

'Let's have a quick look round, then split,' I said. I noticed that I was taking the lead, but Alex, for once, didn't seem to mind. He isn't too bad when we're on our own – well, sometimes, that is. We rummaged around inside the bar and through some drawers and Alex managed to open the wooden money box but there was nothing inside. We searched through the other rooms, then ran up to the one where Mum and Dad were locked in. We shouted through the door.

'There's nobody about but we can't find the key. Sorry. We'll try and get you out.'

'You shove and I'll pull, then,' Dad shouted back.

We pushed. Dad pulled. I could hear him panting furiously, but it was useless. The door was heavy, solid. It was not going to shift. I could hear Mum sobbing on the other side. I took a breather.

Alex. This is horrible!

I knew we'd have to sort it out, kid. And I'm telling you now, we really are caught in a rotten Doctor Who-type time warp. So, kid, we've got to work out how to escape from it . . .

Dad was hissing through the keyhole. 'Do something! Let us out! Or get away and get help!'

Chapter Ten

We stole a look out of a window on to the main street. It was completely deserted.

'There's nobody here.'

'I bet they've all gone off to their Special Day celebrations!'

'We've gotta escape from this horrible place and find someone to help us.'

'Nobody here will help us – they only care about Emmy, not us.'

We ran out into the empty echoing streets, thinking like one person, saying nothing out loud.

Which way?

The one that leads to that castle. That's the way we came in so maybe it's the way we get out of here.

Suppose we run into that awful mist again?

We make our way through it . . .

If poss . . .

And find a policeman . . .

You wish, you wish . . .

Never thought I'd wish to see a policeman . . .

*That's cos you once went shoplifting . . . you would
. . .*

*Shuddup. I never did it again. Come on this way,
kid. I'm sure it's this way . . .*

We ran past the shops with windows like little
black eyes, watching us, frightening. Our feet
pounded over the cobbles, while it felt as if we
were pushing against an invisible force that tried
to hold us back.

You're sure it's this way?

Trust me . . .

*I've never trusted you ever. You've always tried to get
us into trouble . . .*

Well, now I'm trying . . .

To rescue Mum and Dad and find Emmy . . .

I don't give a stuff about Emmy. She's useless . . .

*I hate it when you talk like that. She's lovely and
I'm hoping inside that she's OK.*

Save your hoping for getting through this fog. For here it comes, kid. Come on.

The mist was rolling towards us and suddenly there we were, all wrapped up in a white, fluffy blanket that smothered houses, trees, the road and US.

Grab my hand, kid.

'OK, if you stop calling me THAT. I hate it,' I shouted out loud.

But it's what you are, innit? And if we don't hold hands we'll lose one another and that would be terrible in this. We have to stick together. For always.

You mean I'm stuck with you for EVER? Oh, no, Alex. No, no, no.

Shut up. Just let's keep going!

We struggled on, holding hands, each with the other hand in front of us feeling our way. The mist got into our noses and throats and worst of all, our eyes, blinding us.

'Alex, I'm scared,' I spoke out loud. Right then, I didn't care if anyone heard us.

'Shuddup, you're not. It's me that's scared.'

'I can't see anything.'

We were going slower and slower, fighting our way now through a fog which was so thick it was almost a solid thing.

'We'll never get out of here, Adam!'

'We've got to. Hold on. Don't fall over.'

Too late. We both went down. Somehow we struggled up on to our feet and pushed on, holding hands, not sure any more if we were going the right way, not sure of anything.

'I didn't know hell was a white fog. I thought it was burning flames . . .' Alex muttered through cold almost solid mist.

'I can sort – sort – of see shapes in it. And they look like us!'

'*What* sort of shapes? Only don't tell me. I'm not sure I want to know.'

'Come on, we gotta be brave.'

'I'm not sure courage is in my DNA.'

'Oh come on! They've gone now.'

'Look out! There's a ditch. I'm going into it, it's full of mud – it's HORRIBLE. It's a muddy bank. Help. I'm slipping. And it's the river. Adam! Adam! Help me!'

'I'm here! I've got you! Both hands – I'll pull you out. Come on now!'

'It's squelching. It's holding on to me. Pull, Adam!'

'I am! Now! You pull towards me. Don't pull

me in! That's it. You're OK. OK. You're safe, Alex.'

'You might be safe. I'm soaking. Oh! I hate this place. Please, please, someone up there, let me go home.'

'Don't mention home. I can't bear it. I'm scared we'll be stuck here for ever. It's getting cold. It's lonely here.'

'We've got each other – and – and the mist's getting thinner. Look, look, there's a bridge . . .'

And there was. Looming out of the awful, awful fog . . .

'A beautiful bridgy bridge. I LOVE YOU, BRIDGE. Adam, come on. Let's go over the bridge.'

We ran across the bridge, across the river, through the enemy mist.

'I'm squelching.'

'We both are. Look. We're filthy. We look like . . .'

'Myton Neveridge . . .' we chimed together.

'Suppose it's got us as well . . .'

'The sun's shining now. It'll soon warm us up. Where d'you think we're going?'

'Somewhere far away from here, I hope.'

'But this isn't the way we came in. It's not the way to the castle.'

'Does it matter? It may get us out of here.'

'Out of Myton Neveridge? Oh, I wish, I wish. But it didn't last time, remember.'

'P'raps we'll be lucky this time.'

We ran on, like muddy water rats, but it was getting hot so maybe we'd warm up. Golden clouds appeared in the sky.

The road we were on began to wind uphill. Houses and shops had gone and we were among fields now, out in country. Something appeared on the horizon: could it – could it? – be the castle?

And even as we saw it we became aware of something moving ahead of us like a long snake. We ran faster. We passed an old man hobbling along on sticks, and then a woman carrying a child with two more hanging on to her skirts. Then more and more people. They'd got the Neveridge look, hungry, ragged, and dirty – like us.

'Come on. Something's happening. And we're going to find out what.'

CHAPTER ELEVEN

And now we could see a long chain of people like a gigantic crocodile making its way slowly up the hill towards the castle in the distance. A chain of sad, dreary-looking people, some lame, some bandaged, some blind being led by others. They were pale, tired, withered, no expression on their hopeless faces, only a kind of weary determination to follow whoever was leading them. Children trailed along, not running happily like kids do. As we made our way to the front of this procession I could begin to make out who was at the front of it. Peering hard I thought I could just see the witch leading them, the first time I'd seen her since the crash. And she ... well, she was followed by a very tall man carrying something or someone in his arms.

Could it – could it be Emmy?

I grabbed Alex's arm.

'Watcha doing?'

'They've got Emmy.'

'What can we do about it? Dad just wants us to get away and get help.'

'We can. By following them.'

'I don't want to follow that lot. They won't help us. Suppose they capture us? What use is that gonna be?'

He tried to pull away, but I hung on to him.

'Just let's go with them and see what happens. Then we can try to save Emmy.'

'How?'

'I don't know but we've got to try something, anything.'

'I just want to get away from here . . . let's get away from this lot . . .'

'No, we can't leave Emmy!'

He sighed. 'OK, but it looks hopeless to me.'

We joined the human crocodile, trying not to be noticed. We didn't look much different from the rest. The old castle loomed above us now. All the villagers formed a circle round the ruins and in the middle stood Mr Hanley, the old witch by his side and Emmy in his arms. Quietly we slipped forward then crouched behind one of the mounds to watch. Emmy hung over his hands, thin and little, face pale, golden curls dangling. I ached for her. Little Emmy.

Shut up, thought-waved Alex.

Lord Hanley was speaking,

'I'd just like to say first of all on this momentous day my thanks to Margarita —' a feeble cheer went up as he spoke the name of the witch who was twisting almost writhing beside him — 'who has enabled this special event to take place . . .'

'Margarita, Margarita, Margarita . . .' chanted the villagers like a choir.

' . . . owing to her observation and skill in presenting us with the first opportunity in many years to restore our beautiful, wonderful, lively Lady Eleanor, Queen of the Village, keeper of the Castle . . .'

'Lady Eleanor, Queen of the Village, Keeper of the Castle,' chanted the villagers over and over again.

I looked at Emmy in Hanley's arms. Lively? There was no movement at all. She lay still.

Do you think Emmy's all right?

I dunno. She's either dead or asleep.

That's what I like about you, Alex. You're such a comfort.

Lord Hanley was looking down on her.

'And now that fortune and fate has delivered this beautiful child to us, so like a young Lady Eleanor. Lovely Emmy.'

'Lovely, lovely Emmy. Lovely, lovely, Emmy. Lovely, lovely, Emmy,' went the crowd.

'She can make all our dreams come true and bring Lady Eleanor back to us.'

I was beginning to cotton on to what was going to happen.

He's standing by the tomb we looked at. You remember the letters on it. L, E, Q, V, K, C? Lady Eleanor, Queen of the Village, Keeper of the Castle. And the date on it. August 21st. That's today. The Special Day.

So? Maybe they're just celebrating it like we do Christmas.

But I think they're going to sacrifice Emmy to try and bring Lady Eleanor back to life.

Whatever for?

Cos she's just like her. Maybe they want to turn Emmy into Lady Eleanor or something? What are we gonna do?

Do? I tell you what I'm gonna do. I'm gonna get out of here.

We can't just leave Emmy to be sacrificed!

What else can we do? We can't save her. There's only two of us and hundreds of them! Best thing we can do is get out of here and try and find help.

But they might have sacrificed her by then.

Too bad. There's nothing we can do!

Let's rush into the castle and try and grab her.

You must be joking. Who do you think we are? James Bond doubled? Superman super superman twins? We're only a couple of kids. We can't deal with this.

I can't just go and leave her. It's all right for you. You've never liked her anyway, have you, Alex? You don't care if she dies!

She looks dead already. She's not moving. So there's no point in us getting captured, too.

He would never know how close he'd come to getting his head punched in.

She might just be asleep. Or drugged.

Or she might not be.

You don't care about anybody, do you, Alex?

Yeah, I do. I care about you, Adam. You're my twin — my kid.

No, you don't give a toss. Sometimes I think you only care about computers and things like that. People don't matter to you. You hate Emmy. You hate our cousins.

True. I'm not arguing with you on that one.

And you don't like Mum or Dad, do you?

Oh, shut up. You don't half go on, dontcha? And I tell you what this is really all about, kid. We're in another time, another place, trapped in that mist by some sort of mistake, some accident . . . so we end up in one of those parallel universes we keep hearing about.

No, no, not an accident, it was intended, I'm sure, Alex, because they wanted Emmy . . .

Why would anyone want her? She's useless.

No, you're wrong. She's special. She's what it's all about, Alex, not us. We just happen to be here.

We were so caught up in our mind conversation that we didn't see two figures until we were grabbed from behind. One was Lurch the pub waiter, the other John the wheelmaker. The waiter grinned at Alex, a case of mutual hatred. We struggled and kicked, but it was no good. They tied us up and stuffed our mouths with old, smelly sick-making rags.

'If you're so interested in what's going on

maybe you'd like to take a closer look,' said John.

We were shoved into the ruins of the castle where the strange crowd were engrossed in their bizarre ritual.

'And now this beautiful child's spirit will become one with Eleanor's, her soul will become one with Eleanor's, her life force will become one with Eleanor's, her body and mind will become one with Eleanor's. She will bring her being, her essence, her self . . . .' Lord Hanley's voice was becoming faster and louder. 'Eleanor will be restored back to us in all her former glory . . .'

A strange low humming rose from the villagers gathered round, as the witch weaved to and fro muttering incantations and spells. Slowly the lid of the old tomb seemed to rise in the air. The humming grew louder and louder as the witch lifted up a large jewel-handled dagger and handed it to Lord Hanley where he stood holding Emmy over the grave.

CHAPTER TWELVE

They'd pushed us into a sandy pit under a ruined, half-standing wall where we watched Hanley with the witchy Margarita. Then John and Lurch the waiter left us to join the other villagers who were humming and bowing in their mad ritual. We struggled and kicked and tried to pull at the dirty ropes and smelly gags. Rage rippled through me but Alex's waves of fury were much fiercer, his thoughts black as panthers ready to pounce and destroy. How could they do this to us? How dare they? *I'll kill them all*, Alex screamed at me, *this Lord Hanley and his stinking, rotten, cruel villagers.* His terrible words surged into my mind – Alex had always had more words than anyone in school, always meaning trouble. *I'll obliterate them,*

I'll EXTERMINATE them, he screamed at me. *I'll blast Myton Neveridge off this planet and out of time. How dare it push its runny noses into OUR time! It shouldn't be here with us . . . it doesn't belong here with us . . . it's in another time . . . another place . . . another dimension*

Me: *Maybe we're in theirs.*

Alex: *I don't care which. I just know we've got to sort it . . .*

Me: *But what about Emmy? We've got to save her, Alex!*

Alex: *OK. OK. We'll save your precious Emmy. I promise, Adam. We just need to get free.*

All this time we'd been wriggling, tearing, fighting the gags and ropes, discovering that like everything else in Myton Neveridge they were almost rotten. And Alex, angry to bursting point broke through the decaying ropes and bit through his gag just seconds before I did the same.

Roaring, shouting, he leapt out of the sandy pit and, pulled along on the bond between us, I charged after him, shouting, yelling, glad to be free, wild to save Emmy. The sky seemed to be made of golden metal, the ruined castle silhouetted black against it. Lord Hanley was holding a dagger in one hand and Emmy against him in the other. The droning noise from the villagers grew louder, noisier.

As we ran everything seemed to be in slow motion, my brother Alex a flying figure hurling himself at Hanley, shouting,

'Stop – stop – this can't happen! STOP!'

Right behind him, I yelled, 'Emmy! Emmy! Wake up, Emmy. We're here!'

CHAPTER THIRTEEN

A white cotton-wool ball of mist twists and rolls towards us all, stretching out its spiralling tendons, enveloping the castle and everyone. And out of the white mist Emmy stretches out her arms to a figure wearing a red gown and grey velvety cloak who embraces her before the mist rolls over again obliterating everything, us with it.

CHAPTER FOURTEEN

'What the heck?' exclaimed Alex.

'What the heck?' I said

The creamy stone walls, all new now, not ruined, rose above the surrounding moat and the green grass fields were covered with brightly coloured tents and people and animals and everything you could imagine. A falcon — at least that's what I thought it was — released from a glove, soared into the blue sky. Bells rang. Music played. People sang, talked, laughed. There was noise all over. Happy noise. If these were the villagers of Myton Neveridge, they'd changed, wow, how they'd changed. The summer flowers, springing up every time they were squashed down by feet, bloomed madly everywhere. But I didn't understand . . .

'I don't understand,' said Alex.

'It's our Special Day!' sang out a crowd running past.

'It's our Special Day, so come and play!'

Two girls with flying hair and skirts seized our hands and pulled Alex and me on to paths that ran between stalls selling pies, sweets, flowers, vegetables, fruits, meat, fish, chicken, toys, geese, clothes pegs, and oh, everything . . .

Everything you could never want, Alex thought-waved.

As we hurtled past one of the girls grabbed a garland and threw it over Alex.

'Thou art mine,' she cried. 'I'm Alisoun. Who be ye?'

'Nay, he be mine,' called another voice and Tess grabbed his other hand, and he sent over a despairing wail as he was whirled away. But he was grinning.

'It's *thy* Special Day too,' murmured the girl holding my hand. She was bigger than me and fat and pretty. And she was laughing like crazy as she plonked another garland round my neck. 'What be thee called?'

'Adam,' I answered, as she hauled me along

after the others.

'Then I'm thy Eve,' she cried.

Best of luck, brother, thought-waved Alex.

'I found thee and thee art mine, ye lads,' cried Tess. 'Thou art ours.'

'We're not anybody's,' we both cried.

'Oh! Ye are. It's our Special Day, you see.'

'Come. Dance. Then we taste ALL of it.'

And we did. We watched the jousting, tried the archers, joined in the dancing, watched the mummers, listened to the troubadours, ate sweets and meats, drank strange things that did stranger things to us, flying kites . . . until, exhausted, we collapsed on the flowering grass and watched Punch and Judy, while everyone laughed, shouted and rolled about. For ever, it seemed. Until . . .

Trumpets sounded.

'It's time,' cried Tess, and we were dragged to a grove of trees in front of which stood a tent bigger than the rest, a coloured pavilion, very grand, with a platform at the front of it.

Little girls danced through the trees, carrying baskets out of which they sprinkled rose petals everywhere. They were followed by page boys marching, two of them playing musical instruments, and behind them came four older girls, richly dressed and then through the trees a chair carried by four men holding handles. It was placed on the platform. The four older girls stood round it and Lord Hanley appeared, quite suddenly, tall and stately as ever, a group of villagers behind him. The trumpets and flutes blew a fanfare for . . .

. . . in the chair sat Emmy, in a beautiful embroidered robe, her long golden hair in two plaits and a jewelled band on her head. And everyone knelt down and bowed their heads. I looked around so I did the same.

We've saved her, I thought. *Hanley didn't kill her. She's still alive!*

NO! Alex thought-yelled. *I'm not, not, not going to bow down to Emmy! This lot's all like crazy, but that's the friggin' end!*

Two men started towards him, one of them Lurch, grinning evilly. I stood up as well, to support Alex, I suppose, I dunno. I just know we both stood there among that kneeling crowd like a pair of wallies. More men approached, encircling us, full of menace and grabbed our arms, then forced us down on our knees.

Me: *What, what's happening to us?*

Alex: *A bloomin' parallel universe is what's happening. Must be. Somewhere else. I'm on the REAL planet, I'm playing on the Play Station with you, brother, and we're gonna have burger and chips for supper and Emmy's playing up as usual. At least that's the same here. There she is. Lady Muck. And here's Lord Muck Hanley.*

Lord Hanley lifted both hands in the air.

'Glory Glory Days! have returned to us, for our Beloved Lady, our Queen, is restored to us and we can now look forward to a long future of happiness and prosperity. The dark is behind us, the Waste Land is vanquished and a golden future awaits. We are what we once were for the Lady, Lady Eleanor, our Queen of the Village is here among us once more. Rise up now and rejoice!'

The low humming began again and they all rose to their feet. We were forced to stand up as the villagers chanted:

'Long live the Lady!

'Long live the Lady!

'Long live Queen Eleanor!'

We were dragged to where Emmy sat on the platform, then they pushed us down on our knees again. I could feel Alex's thoughts exploding like an erupting Vesuvius.

'Alex!' I cried.

'Adam!' he replied, 'I'm here!'

'Let them go!' cried Emmy in her kitten miaow voice, just the same as ever (even if they were calling her Lady Eleanor) and clapped her hands. 'They're my funny Alex. My nice Adam. They're my brothers! Emmy loves Alex, Emmy loves Adam.'

I could feel amazement spreading all over Alex. And I knew he'd never given a thought about how Emmy felt about him, only got angry about what he thought of her.

'Just get us out of here, Emmy!' I cried.

'Just get us out of here, Emmy! Please, Emmy!' cried Alex. 'Help us!' The first time he'd ever asked Emmy for help.

The villagers were still chanting,

'Long live the Lady!

'Long live the Lady!

'Long live Queen Eleanor!'

The sound rose in the air, growing louder and louder till it seemed to engulf the great field we were in, the castle and the sky above . . .

Then suddenly once more, the white mist rolled towards us and over us, covering everything like a snowfall in winter.

Alex. Help!

Alex: *Yeah, I'm here.*

Me: *What's happening?*

Alex: *I dunno. I dunno anything any more, but I think it's these worlds colliding – the mist's the gateway – we keep getting trapped by it – we need to get out!*

Me: *Emmy! We've got to get Emmy!*

Alex: *She's OK. I tell you, she's always OK. I can hear something . . .*

Me: *So can I. Something through the mist. Someone speaking.*

Alex: *Yes . . . Voices. They're getting nearer. The mist's clearing. We're coming through, Adam, we're coming through . . .*

CHAPTER FIFTEEN

. . . and we heard the loud booming tones of
larger-than-life Uncle Ben with Aunt Sadie and
cousins Briony, Kelly, Josh and Neville wildly
greeting us like long-lost cousins, which of
course, we were. I gazed round in complete
disbelief. Where was Lord Hanley, the witch and
the villagers? What were Uncle Ben & Co. doing
here? What was going on? My brain was spinning
like a top. Alex was still standing beside me.
Perhaps he knew.

What happened? I asked him.

Don't you know?

No. Do you?

Not really.

Uncle Ben and Aunt Sadie were hugging us. I

never thought I'd be so pleased to see anyone in the whole of my life. Even Alex sounded pleased.

'We were worried when you were later than you said and we couldn't contact you,' said Aunt Sadie, 'so we came to see if we could find you. We knew there was bad fog that day. Then we saw you by the castle ruins.'

'Did you see anybody else apart from us?'

'No, dear. Just you two. And Emmy. What is she doing over there? Lying on the grass? Is she tired or something?'

'Emmy!' Was she OK? I rushed up to her. Please, please, still be alive. She stirred then smiled. She was OK! She'd just been asleep. Hopefully she didn't know what had gone on.

'Hello, Adam,' she said.

With relief flooding through me, I turned to Uncle Ben and Aunt Sadie.

'We'd better go and get Mum and Dad. They're stuck in a place called Myton Neveridge.'

They looked at each other.

'Where? Never heard of it,' said Uncle Ben.

'It's a village just down the road from here. Dad and Mum are there.'

'Yes, we've seen them down the road with your

car. It's broken down, but that doesn't matter. We can take you to the farm in the minibus. There's enough room for everybody. You can fit about twenty people in it,' he said.

All the cousins were running round in the ruins just like Alex and I did the other day. He was trying to avoid Briony who fancies him rotten. Then Mum and Dad arrived.

'Still can't get that car going,' he said.

'Mum, Dad, I thought you were in Myton Neveridge.'

'Where, dear? Never heard of it.'

'He asked us that as well,' said Aunt Sadie. 'Wherever did you get that funny name from?'

'Oh, dunno. Must've seen it on a signpost somewhere.'

So it was just me and Alex who remembered what had happened. I don't think Emmy did since she'd slept through it all. Then I caught his thoughts.

We'd better keep this to ourselves.

Yeah. They won't believe us now. I'm not sure I do in a way. It was like a bad dream, a nightmare.

'Well, we've hung around here long enough now. Sorry we held you up,' said Dad.

'Shall we get going?'

'That's funny. I don't know where the Emmy-mobile has got to,' said Mum.

'Doesn't matter. I'll carry her, then,' said Dad.

But Emmy, who was still sitting on the grass as if she had just woken up, beamed at everyone standing around her and clapped her hands.

'Hello.' She waved and pulled herself up. 'Want to walk.'

'Careful,' said Mum, going towards her. 'Don't fall over.'

Emmy stretched out a leg, then stood up, took an uncertain step, then another, then another.

'Look. Look. I can walk. Walk. Walk. Emmy can walk!'

Everyone stood around watching in disbelief, then:

'That's marvellous, Emmy. How did you manage to do that?' asked Mum.

'You're brilliant, Emmy,' said Briony, kissing her.

It must be something to do with the witch's spell at the tomb, I thought to Alex. *Perhaps instead of Emmy's life going into Eleanor's it's happened the other way.*

Shut up, he replied. *Don't tell ANYONE. We dreamt it – or it was the bumps on our heads. They're pretty bad. But no one else knows so keep quiet! Promise! Or I'll kill you.*

OK, OK, I grinned. *Oh, man, it was so scary.*

So we left the ruined castle, Mum and Dad walking either side of Emmy in case she slipped, but she seemed to be managing OK and we all clambered into the minibus parked by the gate and headed down the road towards Myton Neveridge. But there was nothing there this time. Myton Neveridge had just disappeared, vanished, vamoosed. For ever?

We all drove along in the minibus heading for the farm in high spirits – well, most of us, anyway. Everyone else was chatting away happily except Alex, who was silent. Emmy was the happiest, burbling away, 'I can walk. Walk. Walk.'

We were almost at the farm when she turned to Alex and me and said, 'I nearly wanted to stay there and be a queen. It was nice to be GRAND and have everyone doing what *I* wanted. But they said it meant not seeing you two ever again, not ever, ever, so I came back.'

It was the longest speech she'd ever made. Alex turned to look out of the window.

'What's she talking about?' Mum asked. '*Where* did she come back from?'

'Oh, it's just a game we play sometimes,' I said, for Alex stayed silent.

'Yeah, it's nice to play games, the three of us. Sometimes,' Alex chipped in. I smiled at him.

'You looking forward to seeing the horses again, Emmy?' asked Aunt Sadie.

She clapped her hands.

'Yes. Lovely, lovely, lovely horses.'

And Alex grinned at her.